For Baby Trilliams
~ LW

For my friends
~ JL

CATERPILLAR BOOKS
An imprint of the Little Tiger Group
www.littletiger.co.uk
1 Coda Studios, 189 Munster Road, London SW6 6AW
First published in Great Britain 2019 • This edition puplished in 2020
Text by Libby Walden • Text copyright © Caterpillar Books Ltd 2019
Illustrations copyright © Jacqui Lee 2019
A CIP Catalogue record for this book is available from the British Library
All rights reserved • Printed in China
ISBN: 978-1-83891-008-2 • CPB/1800/1328/1119
10 9 8 7 6 5 4 3 2 1

Libby Walden

Jacqui Lee

This is OWL

Welcome to the wood.

We're here to meet someone very special.

Turn the page and I'll introduce you...

This is... Owl?
Owl? Wake up!

Owl, you're embarrassing me...
this is *not* how we agreed to start the book!

Try tickling Owl's tummy
to wake Owl up.

No, we need both eyes open, Owl.
Your audience is waiting...

Ah! I know!

Owls are nocturnal. That means Owl is
active only during the night-time.

Clap three times to switch off the Sun.

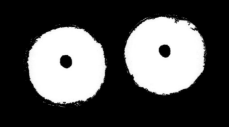

Oops!

Quickly, draw a big, round Moon with
your finger so we can see what's going on.

That's better! Now, let's try again.

This is Owl.
Owl lives in a tree.

But what's the matter, Owl?

No, now is not the time
to be distracted by Beetle!

Okay, okay!
Sorry about this.

Can you tilt the page
to help Owl reach Beetle?

Whoa! You might have
tipped Owl a little too far!

Flap the pages together and
let's get Owl to fly.

Well, quite frankly, you're just
not trying hard enough Owl!

Can you flap the pages a little harder?

Oh dear! Perhaps that was
a little *too* hard that time!

Owl? Where are you going?
You can't just flap off!

Call Owl back with a loud
"twit-twoo!"

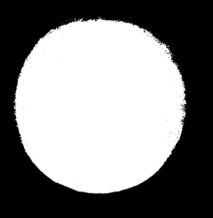

There you are!
And you have a friend.

Wave hello to Other Owl.

Owl, are you trying to build a nest?

But owls don't usually build their own nests...
this could be a disaster!

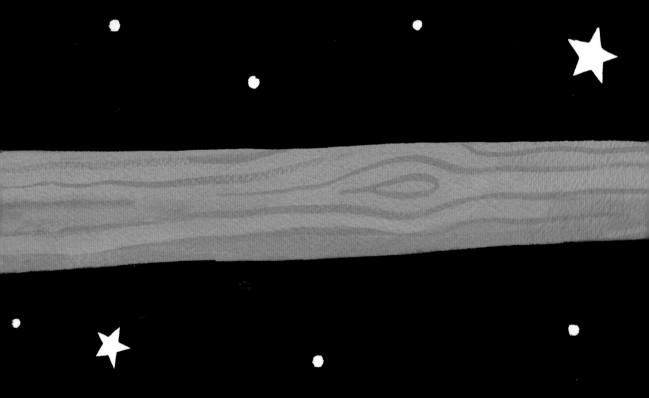

Would you mind lending a hand?

Please draw some twigs with your
finger to help Owl and Other Owl.

There! That's better!

This is the home of Owl and Other Owl.
They look happy, don't they?

Uh-oh! It looks like a raincloud is about
to come and ruin things.

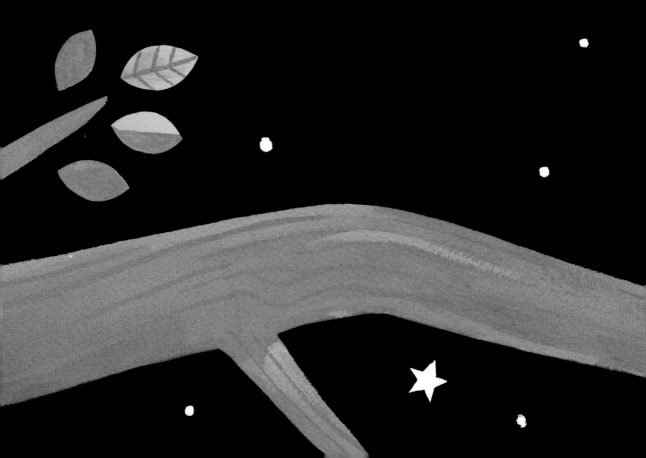

Blow it away, quickly!

What is it Owl?

What do you want to show me?

Let's take a closer look...

What are you hiding, Owl?

You could have cleaned it
before showing it to me!

Sweep away the feathers
and twigs with your finger.

Oh, look!

Welcome to the world, Baby Owl!

Blow Baby Owl a kiss to say hello.

It's almost daybreak in the wood.
Time for owls to go to bed.

Goodnight Owl, Other Owl and Baby Owl.

Can you wave them
a cheery goodbye?

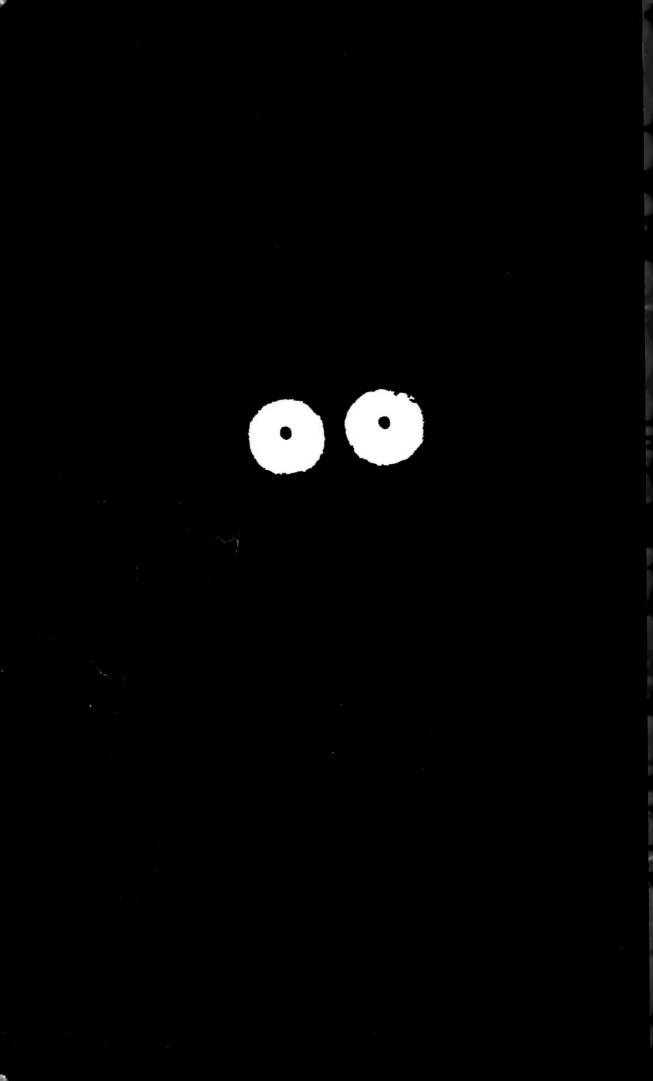